D1524358

ROBIN HOOD & FRIAR TUCK

ZOMBIE KILLERS

A Canterbury Tale

PAUL A. FREEMAN

COSCOM ENTERTAINMENT

WINNIPEG

ISBN 978-1-926712-23-9

PUBLISHED BY COSCOM ENTERTAINMENT
www.coscomentertainment.com
Text set in Garamond
Printed and bound in the USA
COVER ART BY SEAN SIMMANS

Library and Archives Canada Cataloguing in Publication

Freeman, Paul A., 1963-
    Robin Hood and Friar Tuck : zombie killers : a Canterbury
tale / Paul A. Freeman.

Poems.
ISBN 978-1-926712-23-9

    I. Title.

PR6106.R43R62 2009   821'.92   C2009-906169-4

To Kenneth, Deborah, Cathy and Mandy—for encouragement beyond the call of duty. And to those countless internet scribes who make the loneliness of a writer less lonely.

ROBIN HOOD
& FRIAR TUCK
ZOMBIE KILLERS
A Canterbury Tale

Prologue to the Monk's Second Tale

As night drew in, young Geoffrey Chaucer's band
Of pilgrims, sensing darkness was at hand,
Demanded that the next narration told
Should terrify and make the blood run cold.
So at a woodland inn the palmers stopped
And off their carts and weary mounts they hopped.
Then gath'ring in the hostelry they sought
To keep on track their storytelling sport.
They asked for one who'd spread a dose of fear
To frighten them whilst supping wine and beer.

The Monk spoke up to volunteer a tale,
Then putting down a flagon full of ale
Requested that the keeper of the inn
Suppress all boist'rous revelry and din.

"Illuminate this cheerless, brooding room
With candles," added he, "then in the gloom,
Amidst the spooky shadows I shall tell
Of grave events and horrors that befell
The peasants and the gentlefolk who dwelt
Round Nottingham and in the woodland belt
Surrounding that fair town some years ago.

"Yet ere from twixt my lips this tale doth flow
Of Death's reanimations and of days
Spent fighting Satan's devilish malaise,

Allow me to describe the stricken state
Of England when King Richard's sovereign fate
Was hanging in the balance and his lands
Were held, in trust, in crafty Prince John's hands."

The landlord did as bidden to arrange
For candles put in every sconce till strange
And ghostly silhouettes of those arrayed
About the room upon the four walls played.
Then once an air of creepiness was set
The Monk fulfilled his storytelling debt.

Here Beginneth the Monk's Second Tale

Chapter I

Whilst England's brave King Richard was away
In Palestine, embroildèd in the fray
'Gainst Mussulmen to make Jerus'lem home
For Christians and the Holy Church of Rome,
His brother, John, in London hatched a plot
To steal the regent's kingdom and allot
Its fiefdoms to those knights for whom a sop
Of land ensured their loyalty they'd swap.

Their switched allegiance came at dreadful cost
To those who tilled in sun, and rain, and frost
And through their labors kept the clergy clothed;
For by their Norman lords these serfs were loathed,
Disparaged for their lowly Saxon birth—
Condemning them to turn the thankless earth.

The barons and the abbots levied tax
Upon these needy workers, filling sacks
With coinage made of silver and of gold;
Then one stood up against them, one so bold,
That on his head was placed a large reward—
As much as his detractors could afford.

This hero's name was Robin of the Hood;
He harried nobles riding through the wood
Round Nottingham, then shared the pilfered gains
With those who bore the Normans' binding chains.
He gave this stolen bounty to the poor,
Indifferent to Prince John's stringent law
And hoped there'd be a pardon in the air
Once Richard sat again upon the chair
Of sovereignty and distanced from the throne
His brother with the heart as cold as stone.

Though Robin had adventures by the score,
Enough to fill a manuscript or more,
Not one could match the time our honest champ
And several of his men unearthed a camp
Hid deep within the forest by a stream.

Upon a skewer lay a roasting bream,
Yet ere the hungry group of outlaws fell
Upon the fish, young Much decried a bell.

"This mournful sound foreshadows naught but ill!"
The miller's son called out. "So hold ye still.
Taste not this stranger's food, nor touch his things,
Since round his neck the leper's warning rings."

An owlish hoot from Scarlet Will curtailed
All further talk, for in the woods travailed
The figure of a Friar from whom the knell
Rang ominously through the verdant dell.

"Before we panic," whispered Robin Hood,
"Let's learn if this lone priest means ill or good."

With this the outlaw company concealed
Their whereabouts, then suddenly revealed

Their presence once the cloaked and hooded Friar
Had placed a heap of branches by his fire.

Emerging from amongst the forest trees
Like autumn leaves upon the Sherwood breeze,
The bandits formed a ring around their prey—
A portly man whose threadbare cape of gray
Was pitted full of holes bespeaking wear.
He shed his hood, revealing tonsured hair
And features bronzed and burnished by the sun—
As brown as is an Easter hot-crossed-bun.
Yet florid were his cheeks, with veins of red,
Which told on beer and wine he'd often fed.

"My name," the man announced, "is Friar Tuck,
And trusting to the will of God and luck,
I seek one Robin Hood, for in this shire
A weird contagion soon shall spread like fire
Amongst the Sheriff's men, creating strife,
Then bringing those infected back to life."
And pointing to his leper's bell, he said,
"Although this trinket might attract the dead
It keeps away that murd'rous knight named Guy
Who brought this dreaded sickness from the dry
And dusty lands where Richard now crusades—
From one of our unholy, bloody raids."

Incredulously, Robin viewed the monk
And wondered if perchance the man was drunk.
"You've sought and now discovered me," he said.
"Yet seemingly within your mind you've bred
Some fantasies which urged you root me out,
So tell me what this story's all about."

Ere Friar Tuck could tell his baffling news
A man came blund'ring through a stand of yews.

5

Not clad in Lincoln green like Robin's men,
But in the Sheriff's livery, and then,
With fevered eye and chomping jaws assailed
The outlaw Will, whose arms like windmills flailed
In vain to stop this unprovoked attack.
The soldier's teeth bit deeply in the back
Of Scarlet's neck, and ripped away some flesh.
He chewed as if the morsel were a fresh
And juicy piece of venison or steak,
Then on Will's spurting blood he strove to slake
His appetite, and satisfied his thirst.

To Scarlet's rescue, Robin was the first.
And though the interloper took a knife
Between the ribs it didn't end the life
Of this infernal denizen from Hell.
But finally the vicious monster fell
When Friar Tuck pulled back his cloak and drew
A sword with which the evil beast he slew.
"A stabbing's not enough!" the Friar said,
And with one blow cut off the creature's head.

As Will bled out and gasped, and breathed his last
The Sherwood men stood silent and aghast,
Their shocked expressions filled with disbelief
That men could treat their kin as chunks of beef
Like meat to fuel the body and sustain
That force of Life ingested foods maintain.
Then suddenly the corpse of Scarlet stirred
As if his limbs and torso hadn't heard
About his premature and brutal end.

"My loyal servant's mortal hurt doth mend,"
Cried Robin, rushing over to embrace
The rousing man, then noticed that his face
Was pale as death, with bared and gnashing teeth.

"Beware!" the Friar shouted. "For beneath
Your friend's pretense of life, he's now a beast
Which on your flesh and blood intends to feast."
And with these words of warning Friar Tuck
Once more raised up his keen-edged sword and struck,
Decapitating Will with one deft stroke.

Young Much, his dagger drawn, prepared to poke
His blade into the monk's expansive chest
Till Robin told the lad, "It's for the best.
This creature only bore Will Scarlet's guise.
'Tis mercy that we've witnessed his demise
And liberated Will's immortal soul."

So once the band had made a shallow hole
In which to place their comrade till a grave
Could be arranged, the holy Friar gave
A full account of how this weird disease
That seemingly reanimates with ease
Its victims came to reach the English shores.

"This illness which defies all natural laws,"
Said Friar Tuck, "was brought from distant climes,
A penalty, perhaps, for wicked crimes
Committed by our own crusading knights
Against the local people's human rights.
So since poor Scarlet's grave has now been dug,
I'll tell you how this strange and fatal bug
Originated in those foreign lands,
To punish our crusaders' bloody hands.
Without ado, to you I shall impart
My story from its inoffensive start."

And this Tuck did, for here is what he said
About reanimation of the dead:

"When Richard called the country's knights to arms,
His noblemen enlisted from their farms
A soldiery of serfs to go abroad,
To fight against the brutal Muslim horde.
Then priests who might perform the final rites
Required by God were hired by these knights
To minister to those with wounds so grave
Their lives were deemed impossible to save.

"Amongst these chosen clergymen was I,
Recruited for that ruffian Sir Guy
Of Gisborne, who for Nottingham did ride
Against the Turks, accomp'nied by his bride
The lady, Claire—a wicked, heartless lass
Who hoped upon this trip she might amass
A wealth of pilfered silver, gems and gold.

"The Abbott of St. Mary's Abbey told
Myself and all my colleagues that he planned
To send unto the blessèd Holy Land
A brother under Guy's protective wing.
And since my voice was often heard to ring
With stories of the Abbot's thieving ways
'Twas I on whom he set his haughty gaze.

"When due to leave, the Sheriff came along
Upon his horse to give the martial throng,
And Guy, his nephew, such a stirring speech
That once we stepped upon a sandy beach
In Palestine, each man would gladly kill
The Saracens and do the Church's will.

"The climate of the Holy Land proved hot,
The sun a harsh and unrelenting blot
Of brightness burning down on us all day

Till nighttime took its punishment away.
And even when the desert sun was hid
Behind infrequent clouds this couldn't rid
The air of its inherent daytime heat.

"Our infantry was swaying on its feet
From hunger and from thirst until the stamp
Of marching feet was halted at the camp
Of lion-hearted Richard and his men.

"The English king received us at his den,
And said, 'Although this climate's barely fit
For Christian folk, a mighty weight doth sit
Upon our shoulders, urging us to beat
The Turkishmen and violently unseat
The tribal chiefs who plague this holy place.
So gird your loins, dear countrymen, and brace
Yourselves to do the work of God and spill
The pagans' blood until you've had your fill.'

"His speech brought forth a long and rousing cheer
And banished from our breasts the gnawing fear
Of being in an unfamiliar land.
'Sir Guy,' said Richard, 'take your gallant band
Of Englishmen and lead them to the east
Where at a far oasis lives a beast,
A local warlord dubbed the Dark Caliph,
An arrogant and condescending thief
Who under your compulsion shall refrain
From fleecing those who enter his domain.'

"On hearing this, Sir Guy and Lady Claire
Smiled broadly, though our regent cautioned care.
'This Dark Caliph,' warned Richard, 'takes advice
From one believed to practice for a price
The evil arts by raising up the dead,

Whom on the flesh of living folk are fed.
This mercenary Necromancer's clout
Must be undone before you dare to rout
His master's troops and take his desert lair.'

"These words of warning didn't temper Claire
Nor Guy of Gisborne's spirit and resolve.
For Richard had permitted them to solve
With deadly force this problem to the east,
No matter if the number of deceased
Amongst the civil populace was high.

"'It seems that with impunity,' said Guy,
'The soldiers of our military mob
May terrorize the countryside and rob
The peasantry; for Richard gives us leave
Through careless words to terrorize and thieve.'

"To celebrate, Sir Guy broke out the ale
The night before we ventured to assail
The stronghold where this enemy held out,
Empowered by his necromancing lout.

"Our army reveled deep into the night,
Then gathered in the morning set to fight."

Chapter II

"So, flaunting the Crusaders' noble code
Of chivalry, we started on the road
To where the Dark Caliph had built his fort.
And on the way the soldiery made sport
Of merchants and of pilgrims and their kin.
They severed limbs, but firstly flayed the skin
From victims to discover where they kept
Their valu'bles, yet though my conscience wept,
My loyalty remained with Holy Rome.

"Oh how I wish I'd never left my home
In England with her forests and her trees;
Her rain, her snow and gentle, cooling breeze.
Yet even as the body count increased,
And though I prayed to God to be released
From Guy's command, the nightmare wouldn't end
Of slayings which no Christian should defend.

"At last, once countless innocents were killed
And Gisborne's coffers nearly had been filled
With looted wealth from blameless, Muslim folk,
Our thirsty, dehydrated soldiers broke
Their serried ranks and ran towards a spot
Of distant green, like arrows newly shot.
Amongst the Dark Caliph's oasis springs
We swooped as if upon our feet were wings,
And by the verdant palms we slacked our thirst

Until our tautened bellies almost burst.

"When sated, Gisborne's army looked about
And saw our foe's formidable redoubt.
The walls were high and thick, but made of earth,
Which caused our men a goodly deal of mirth.

"'This bastion, of muddy, sun-baked bricks,'
Said Guy, 'will not resist those knightly tricks
Employed to guarantee a winning siege.
The plaudits of our lion-hearted liege
Are mine unless our plans should go askew—
Alas, this day, the Dark Caliph shall rue.'

"We camped where this oasis met a sea
Of desert sand, a place where we were free
To look upon the fortress from the dunes.

"'The Necromancer needn't read his runes,'
Laughed Lady Claire, 'to know the end is nigh.'
Yet little did we know the rolling die
Of Fate would fall against our grand designs
And test the oaken stoutness of our spines.

"From up above, whilst setting up our camp,
We watched the local population tramp
From mud brick homes to sturdy fortress gate,
To beg admittance lest they meet the fate
Of those we'd killed and robbed upon the way
To meet our foe in soldierly affray.

"'This influx of civilian refugees,'
Said Guy, 'will bring the fortress to its knees.
For soon their stocks of food will be consumed,
And then, without a morsel, they'll be doomed.
The specter of starvation is our friend,

To bring this siege more promptly to an end.'

"Upon the fortress ramparts soon we saw,
A garrison of troops prepared for war.
In chain-mail coats, with arrows and with bows
They took their place to slay their Christian foes.
And striding midst his troops the Dark Caliph
Was seen instilling pluck and self-belief.
The Necromancer by his master stood,
A frowning dwarf whose face was set like wood,
Reciting from his rigid lips a spell
Inspired by demonic imps from Hell.

"We started preparations straight away
To lay a siege, our spirits bright and gay.
For mustering upon the rampart wall
Were just one hundred troops to stop the fall
Of this, the Dark Caliph's oasis den.

"Sir Guy's first task was ordering some men
To guard the points of egress from the fort
So any persons fleeing might be caught.
The rest were sent abroad to cut down trees,
Since bringing holed up soldiers to their knees
Required rams for splintering the gate
And catapults to undermine the state
Of buttresses, and walls of mud and earth.

"From nearby hills, to overcome a dearth
Of suitable projectiles we brought rocks
And next to every catapult placed stocks
Of heavy stones to batter down the walls.
Yet when these weapons answered to the calls
To lob their loads, they made no single dent
And soon our ammunition had been spent.

"Sir Guy and Lady Claire were sorely vexed,
And rumor said our mission had been hexed.
'The Necromancer's placed on us a curse!'
Our soldiers said, and making matters worse
Our ram proved ineffectual as well,
The victim of another magic spell
Which made the wooden gate seem strong as steel.
The batt'ring ram we drove with manly zeal
Upon its eight-wheeled chassis 'gainst the door,
And when it struck, a loud victorious roar
Exploded from each English soldier's mouth,
Not knowing that our plans were heading south.
The beam of cedar splintered as it crashed
Against the gate which stayed intact, un-smashed.
And those poor souls who pushed the shattered beam
Were decimated by a scalding stream
Of boiling water poured from up above.

"Observing this, Guy threw his steely glove
Upon the ground and stamped his feet and swore.
'There'll be,' said he, 'a settling of the score
With this unholy wizard,' so he fetched
An expert bowman, Hubert, who had fletched
His arrows with the feathers of a goose
To make them fly more truly when let loose.

"'Ascend the nearby hills,' commanded Guy,
'And from your eyrie let an arrow fly
To pierce the Necromancer's evil heart.
Then once you've done our business with your dart
The walls of this invincible redoubt
Will tumble 'neath the weight of English clout.'"

Chapter III

"So Hubert left to climb the tallest hill,
His quiver full, to act on Gisborne's will.
Yet as he clambered upwards, one of Guy's
Commanders had some feedback from his spies.
'The ramparts of the fortress still are filled
With archers, though two score of them we've killed
With arrows and with catapulted stones
Which pierced their mortal flesh and splintered bones.
So lest the Dark Caliph conceals reserves
Within his walls, the soldiery that serves
Upon the lofty battlements is manned
With those reanimated by the hand
Of wizardry, for verily they're stale
In stench, with facial features deathly pale.'

"Incredulously Guy and Lady Claire
Looked out towards their rival's earthen lair,
And sure enough, some troops seemed unlike men;
As if entranced, they moved no muscle when
An English arrow winged its way by luck
And in their leaden bodies firmly stuck.

"Yet of this strange phenomenon a more
Macabre account would frighten to the core
Us Englishmen on Hubert's swift return—
A tale so grim, it made our stomachs churn.

"Said Hubert, 'From the hills I oversaw
The sweeping panorama of our war.
But notably, below me, in the square
Between the fortress walls upon the bare
And open ground, civilians quaked in fear.
The reason for their terror soon was clear;
For some amongst our enemies were hit
So badly that their carcasses were fit
For nothing but the graveyard or a pyre.
Yet rather than an earthy hole or fire
To temper their corruption, they were still
Alive, although divested of their will.
The Necromancer, 'neath the fortress walls,
Directed their activities with calls
To notch an arrow's shaft, or string a bow
Before they let their deadly missiles go.'

"'Yet worse was still to come, since to sustain
This legion of the dead and thus maintain
The number of our foes the wizard fed
The peasants to the ravenous undead.
Those villagers by ropes and chains were bound
To stakes which left them tethered to the ground
And easy prey for every famished beast,
Like morsels at a ghoulish monster's feast.
The undead soldiers, taking some respite
From sharing in their warlord's desp'rate fight,
Would circle the civilians and tear
Their arms and legs from sockets till the air
Was filled with sprays of bright arterial blood
That stained the stronghold's grounds and left a flood
Of scarlet fluid running on the floor.

"Excited by the gruesome sight of gore,
These hellish automatons gathered round
Their victims with a hungry growling sound

To chew their severed limbs or gouge deep ruts
Into their stomachs, accessing the guts
Of twitching prey whilst those surviving cried
In anguish at their kith and kin who'd died.'

"'Once satisfied, these strange corporeal ghosts,
With shuffling steps returned unto their posts
To join their living brethren in the fray.
Methinks that at the battlements they stay
To notch and fletch their arrows and to stretch
Their bowstrings ere they eat another wretch.
These monsters are the soldiery which serves
To constitute the Dark Caliph's reserves.'

"Once Hubert had recounted the abuse
These ghouls dished out, he ventured an excuse
For not assassinating he whose skill
In arts of darkness raised the dead to kill
And mutilate those helpless refugees.

"Said Hubert, 'Though there was no desert breeze
To turn aside my arrow from its course,
My mind was much affected by the force
Of what occurred below my lofty nest.
It put my powers sorely to the test.
My steady hands at once began to shake
On seeing what repast these ghouls partake.

"'Whilst living corpses fought our troops or fed
(Their jaws besmirched with gore, their clothes stained red),
Directing operations from below,
The Necromancer showed them where to go.
And though the dwarfish, black magician stood
Immobile, like a target made of wood,
My heart was beating fast, my brow was hot,
And due to this I couldn't take my shot.'

"Sir Guy was still incredulous and yelled,
'For duty's dereliction you are held
Responsible; such lies I've never heard.
You lost your nerve and failed to fell our bird.
For this, your crime, you'll swing before the crowd.'

"'My Lord!' cried Hubert, 'though no arrow plowed
Into the Necromancer's flesh I swear
That given one more chance my shaft will tear
Into this imp, unto its feathered plume.'

"This promise seemed to lift Sir Gisborne's gloom
Till Gilbert Black, an archer from the heart
Of Africa, stepped forward to impart
Some knowledge of these brutal ghouls now rife
Who seemed to be ensnared twixt death and life.

"'The living dead,' said he, 'are brought about
By wizardry, and though I sense your doubt,
I guarantee such creatures do exist
Which though deceased continue to persist
To do their master's bidding and his will.
These monsters known as 'zombies' need to fill
Their bellies with the warm and tender meat
Of human prey, and when they are replete
They're often put to work to till the fields
To toil for free, augmenting farmers' yields.'

"Convinced at last that zombies were a fact,
Sir Guy decided how 'twas best to act.
'The only way,' said he, 'that we might beat
The Dark Caliph is if we can defeat
The magic of his necromancing chum.
So when next time I hear the telltale hum
Of Hubert's arrow whizzing to its mark,

I hope it shall engulf the mortal spark
That burns within that devil's evil breast.
Then once his shaft hath pierced the wizard's chest,
Our batt'ring ram will raze the fortress door,
And catapulted stones will strike and bore
Beyond the flimsy fabric of the fort.
But mostly, when he's dead, we'll have some sport
In culling zombies once their puppeteer
Has fallen to our Hubert's deadly spear.'"

Chapter IV

"So once again our soldiers set about
Designing more contraptions built to rout
Our enemies and bring a rapid end
To this unholy sideshow, then we'd spend
The remnants of the ghastly Great Crusade
With Richard, camped inside his palisade.

"The troops cut down more trees and made a ram,
A solid beam of wood we hoped would slam
Against the fortress gate and break apart
An aperture through which our men could dart.
We also fetched replenishments of rocks,
Enough to fill the atmosphere with flocks
Of pelting stones once catapults let fly
Their loads into the burning desert sky.

"Yet just to guarantee a strong assault
(Enough to bring resistance to a halt),
Sir Guy commanded wooden ladders built
To scale the fortress walls and swing the tilt
Of fortune in this curious campaign
To end the Dark Caliph's malignant reign.

"But ere we might bombard and then attack
This bastion protected by the black,
Unholy wizard, first we had to floor
This man bewitching fortress walls and door

Which weathered our projectiles and our ram,
By slaughtering the villain like a lamb.

"To this grim end, our archer, Hubert, scaled
The nearby hills, and knowing if he failed
The gallows called, he drew a steady bead
And stretched his bow to do the fatal deed.

"My part in operations was to pray
To God that we might raze those walls of clay
Like Jericho's, then smite our rivals dead
And sever with our swords each zombie's head.
I begged the Father, Son and Holy Ghost
To aid us, ere dispensing wine and host.
On top of this, the catapults I blessed,
Before we put their aim unto the test.
The batt'ring ram, I sanctified as well,
To help defeat those powers loosed from Hell.

"As for myself, a tubby, peaceful monk
Who ate too much and often got too drunk
To stand up straight, 'twas time to show some pluck
And make a name for Friar Michael Tuck.

"I found myself a trusty chain mail shirt
And to my waistband resolutely girt
A sword, whilst in my hand I placed a rod—
A quarterstaff—to give our foes a prod.
A helmet made of steel to shield my skull,
Completed my attire ere the cull
Of enemies, in earnest, should begin
To cleanse this desert outpost of its sin.

"With preparations truly underway,
Our bowman, Hubert, geared himself to slay
The Necromancer, waiting for the nod

From Gisborne—and the guiding hand of God.

"The signal from Sir Guy was soon supplied,
For stood upon the battlements he spied
The Dark Caliph and black magician out
Amongst the troops, obliterating doubt
And urging those both living and undead,
Hold out and put this Christian siege to bed.

"On seeing Gisborne's gesture, Hubert let
His arrow fly upon its deftly set
Trajectory, until the skillful shot
Struck home and pierced the wizard's mortal spot.
His heart was cleaved in two, and though he cried
In shock, an instant later he had died.

"The moment that the wizard hit the floor,
The English troops let out a mighty roar.
Cried Gisborne, 'By Our Lady and St. George,
'Tis time for us on heathen blood to gorge
Our appetites, so let's begin the fight
By putting streams of arrows into flight.'

"A feathered shaft was loosed from every bow
While catapults were readied for a throw.
And when these great contraptions lobbed their rocks
They took the fortress walls apart with blocks
So large dislodged that through the holes a man
Might pass—and so the main attack began.

"'The wizard's foul enchantment is curtailed,'
Yelled Guy, and hearing this our troops assailed
The fortress with the batt'ring ram out front.
The gate, once so unyielding, took the brunt
And smashed to smithereens within its frame.

"We raised a cheer, yet wondered why a tame,
Desultory fire was all the Dark Caliph
Could muster, for resistance had been brief.
A single volley only had they sent
Of arrows, then their rows of archers bent
Their bows no more, which left our army free
To cross the dang'rous intervening sea
Of open ground twixt English lines and fort.
Yet no protracted arrow fire was brought
To bear whilst we advanced upon our prize,
And soon 'twas clear the fortress would be Guy's."

Chapter V

"Amongst our eager infantry I charged
And through the gate, now pulverized, I barged.
To sword and arrow foes about me fell,
And when my nose discerned the awful smell
That hung upon the air, I then recalled
The sight that Hubert saw which so appalled
His senses and had caused his hands to shake.

"The spectacle about us made us quake,
For seemingly that moment when we stole
The wizard's life, his magic lost control
Not only of the bastion walls and gate,
But also of the living soldiers' late,
Lamented friends he'd lifted up from death.
With scratching claws, with biting teeth and breath
So fetid that it made our stomachs retch,
These mindless, hungry beasts now strove to fetch
The human flesh they needed to survive
From those amongst their colleagues still alive.

"Upon the ramparts, desperate struggles raged.
The undead brutes, like vicious beasts un-caged
Attacked their fellows, ripping out their throats
As if their friends were sacrificial goats,
Then gathered round and drank the spurting blood,
Exalting in the red, arterial flood.
And once the shuffling creatures had their fill,

They used their raking fingernails to spill
The innards of their victims on the floor.
Around these piles of steaming guts and gore
The zombies crouched and ate until a new
Unsullied victim came into their view;
And then the lumb'ring army of the dead
Would leave the livid corpse on which they fed
To go in search of fresher, pristine meat.

"And finally the zombies closed to eat
The man they'd called till recently their chief,
Their overlord, the so-called Dark Caliph.
His bodyguards they swiftly overcame
By weight of numbers, though the men were game
And waged a frantic battle for their lives.
Against these beasts they fought with swords and knives,
But one by one these bodyguards were felled,
And by the hungry, undead corpses held
Immobile on the ground till teeth bit deep
And hands like claws scooped out a bloody heap
Of entrails for a monster's tasty feast.

"The last to meet his end, but not the least,
Upon those tainted battlements was he
Who'd let the necromancing fiend set free
The power to reanimate a man
Whose life had run its predetermined span.
The garrison of ghouls from every side
Surrounded the Caliph and ere he died
They bit and scratched and tore his yielding flesh,
Then lapped at blood still flowing through his mesh
Of arteries and veins until the strain
Upon his heart curtailed his mortal pain.

"'By grim default,' cried Guy, 'the day is ours.
And though we're stunned, no English soldier cowers

Or shies away from God's intended task.
So even if afraid, I urge you mask
Your fear and put these demons to the sword.
For next we'll rummage round and find the hoard
Of treasure which the Dark Caliph keeps stashed
Inside this eerie fortress where we've clashed.'

"The number of the living dead was few,
So eagerly we minded Gisborne's cue.
The promise of a fortune had us spurred
To action, then we noticed someone stirred
Amongst our men who'd fallen in the heat
Of battle when a zombie stripped the meat
About his neck, from which a squirting gout
Of blood ensured him swiftly bleeding out.

"'The newly dead are rising up as well!'
I cried. 'So add the soldiery that fell
By scratch and bite to those we need to kill.
For even though they're lying deathly still
A strange infection's running through their veins
Which brings them back to dine upon the brains,
And viscera and flesh of those alive.'

"And as I spoke, some more appeared to thrive,
Whom we had slain, or else were put to death
By monsters who had sucked their final breath
Before the Necromancer met his end.

"Said Gilbert Black, 'If we're to now defend
Ourselves against this menace, 'tis well known
In Africa that if you take a stone
And dash a zombie's brains out, then it dies
And lies inert to feed the frenzied flies.'
So turning to Sir Guy he made a plea:
'Before through force of numbers we must flee,

Bring up your lordship's armouror and then
Select those blades and bludgeons for your men
With which we might defeat this evil foe
By aiming at their heads a fatal blow.'

"Sir Guy agreed, and buying us some time
(As from the ramparts beasts began to climb
Intent on further carnage) he denied
His soldiers leave to have the folk untied
On whom till now the zombie horde had fed.
And even though those blameless peasants pled
For clemency, our lord remained unmoved.

"Unluckily, this callous tactic proved
A two-edged sword; for soon the undead swelled
Their numbers with the villagers they felled
And brought into their ranks by tooth and nail.

"So though it seemed our policy might fail
(For we were next upon the list of prey),
We faced those beasts, our features drawn and gray.
But trusting God, we gallantly held back
With sword and staff the creatures' first attack,
Now knowing that the simplest scratch or bite
Transmitted this repulsive, deadly blight."

Chapter VI

"Yet just as circumstances seemed quite bleak
The armouror arrived with tools to wreak
Upon these creatures injuries most grave,
Which rallied us and made our men feel brave.
Though I was armed with quarterstaff and sword
To strike the undead down and cut the cord
That tethered them to this, the living world,
We now had metal flails round which was twirled
A spike-encrusted ball upon a chain,
And maces made of steel to crush the brain.
These bludgeons were augmented with the blades
Of axes, sharpened hammers and of spades
With which a swift and well-aimed strike could deck
These creatures, separating from the neck
The noggin, thus ensuring them deceased.

"So ere we joined the menu of their feast,
On our own terms we faced our deadly foe,
Delivering at first a crucial blow
By striking our opponents from the rear.
For this assault we used untested gear—
The ladders we had built to scale the walls
If missile fire were swapped for desperate brawls.

"Abruptly troops held in reserve appeared
Upon the lofty battlements and speared
What zombies still remained before they crushed

Their skulls until their famished groans were hushed.
Then once these ghoulish laggards had been trounced,
On those inside the courtyard square they pounced.
This left our undead adversaries snared,
Encircled with their gnashing teeth prepared
To banquet on crusaders' tender meat
Until their growling bellies were replete.

"And as for me, I'd joined the fearless band
Of Gisborne's men who'd made a noble stand
Beside the gate round which the zombie swarm
Descended in the hopes they'd taste our warm
And salty flesh before we got rearmed.
But with our newfound weaponry we calmed
Their appetites by charging at their ranks,
Whilst those who'd scaled the walls attacked their flanks.

"From outside—working in—we fought our way,
The undead hunters now the hounded prey.
My quarterstaff resounded with a dull,
Traumatic thud each time it crushed a skull,
Whilst at my side a young lieutenant's mace
Swung left and right at any rabid face
That came within the distance of his arm.
The flails were also harbingers of harm,
Their sundry barbs transforming brains to paste.
The bladed weapons too received a taste
Of blood and gore—the battleaxes swung
So skillfully that many heads soon hung
From threads of flesh or rolled upon the floor.
Our sharpened hammers burrowed to the core
Of many rotten brains, whilst with a spade
Decapitation saw the monsters laid
Out dead, their skulls caved in or cleaved in two,
Their carcasses a pallid, deathly hue.

"Yet all was not straightforward as it seemed,
For with each blow the blood of zombies streamed
In fountains from their wounds and stained the ground,
And bits of bloodied meat flew all around
Discoloring our tunics and our skin
Where cuts might let the vile infection in.

"At first we clearly realized who was who—
The Dark Caliph's own soldiers and the few
Reanimated refugees we'd left
Secured to stakes and grievously bereft
Of hope were those 'gainst whom we had to fight
And with our blades and bludgeons firmly smite.

"Yet gradu'lly survival's odds were stacked
Against ourselves, for some of us were wracked
With fever, till the body fast succumbed
As arms, then hands, then fingers swiftly numbed
Unto this strange contagion of the dead.

"At first we thought Sir Guy had deftly led
Our gallant men to victory, but soon
A soldier at my feet, a vicious goon
Who'd ventured to the middle of the fray
And fallen 'neath the zombies in a spray
Of spurting scarlet blood began to rise,
The madness of the undead in his eyes.

"This victim's ilk we rapidly dispatched,
But now we noticed even those men scratched
Or bitten had the poison in their veins.
It paled their skin and slowly dulled their brains
Till all at once their hearts gave out and stopped
And to the floor their lifeless bodies flopped.
Yet lifeless they were not, and if by blade
Or club reanimation wasn't stayed,

They rose and carried on the evil work
Created by the necromancing Turk.

"Alas it seemed for every zombie's head
We severed, one more man rose up undead
To take his place, to even up the score
Of those alive and those who broke the law
Of nature which dictates that once the heart
Gives out, the soul's long journey ought to start.

"The frantic fight for life was touch and go,
As loyal friend transformed to deadly foe
And needed to be slaughtered ere he might
Infect the uninfected with his bite.
Amongst the carnage only I remained
And Gilbert Black, who with his mace had brained
The last resurgent corpse, whilst from the gate
Sir Guy of Gisborne looked upon his late
Lamented army lying in a heap,
Amidst their foes, in everlasting sleep.
Then on her horse the Lady Claire arrived
With Hubert, making five who had survived
The Necromancer's spell to resurrect
A garrison of ghouls he might direct
In battle 'gainst Sir Guy's crusading band
To save the Dark Caliph's oasis land.

Chapter VII

"Said Lady Claire, 'Perhaps it's for the best
So many died, for when we find the chest
Of treasure, there's but five to share the wealth.'
Then moving room to room with haste and stealth,
She searched the fortress quarters till she found
A chamber which contained a looming mound
Of jewelry, of silver, gems and gold.

"'It's here!' the avaricious lady told
The world, her eyes alight, and as we four
Rushed in to see, a shape behind the door
Emerged with chomping jaws and ravaged face,
Its arms extended, hoping to embrace
Guy's greedy spouse to feast upon her meat.

"Before the shambling figure could deplete
Her tender flesh, I swung my trusty sword
And where a head once sat, a geyser poured
Into the air and dyed the chamber red.
The headless man fell forward ere he'd fed,
His hands held out, then toppled on his prey
And tainted her with bright arterial spray.

"In shock we viewed the head upon the floor,
The staring eyes, the bloody, open maw.
And on the face the features of the man
Who'd tried to make Guy's lady join the clan
Of undead beasts by hiding like a thief

Was he—the Necromancer's Dark Caliph.

"'In death,' said I, 'this man still guards his wealth.
Yet how can gold restore a zombie's health?
The force of life within him has been lost.
For dire defeat he's paid an awful cost.'

"Sir Guy took Lady Claire outside to clean
The zombie's blood away and once he'd seen
His wife was not the worse for her ordeal
They both returned, relieved my blade of steel
Had stopped the savage monster in its tracks.

"Whilst I, the 'Fighting Friar,' watched their backs
The others loaded saddle bags with loot
To smuggle back to England on the route
By land and sea that held the smallest threat
Of being snared within a brigand's net
Or asked to give our spoils to Richard's band
To fund his exploits in this bone-dry land.

"We moved our bags of booty to the cart
Belonging to the armouror whose heart
Was plundered from his ribcage whilst it beat
And eaten like a tasty cut of meat
By those undead who now composed a heap
Of corpses seized in everlasting sleep.

"At first I wasn't certain that our pact
To split the warlord's booty was an act
That God would sanction till I thought it out,
Expunging from my mind my nagging doubt.
For mine own share would be a double tithe—
One fifth—enough to help the folk who writhe
With hunger in the English countryside,
Near Nottingham, the place where I reside."

Chapter VIII

"By circumventing Richard and his men
We made our way to Antioch, and then
Embarked upon a ship which took us west,
To Malta, past Gibraltar, on to Brest,
Till finally, at Dover she arrived.
However, not all five of us survived
The journey, though it started well enough.

"The wind was brisk, the sea a little rough,
But in our round-hulled boat with single sail
We hugged the coast, so if a dang'rous gale
Blew up we could at once put in to port
Or flee from pirates ere our ship were caught.
The crew (a coarse and vicious-looking bunch
Of ruffians), although they had a hunch
Our cargo was of value turned a blind
Unseeing eye for Guy of Gisborne lined
Their pockets to ensure they wouldn't snoop
Or meddle in the dealings of our group.

"But then Sir Guy announced to us the share
Of treasure that himself and Lady Claire
Were claiming shouldn't equal that which I
And Gilbert Black and Hubert might rely
On getting once we reached the English shore.

"'My Lady and myself deserve much more,'
He said, 'for we are both of noble birth,
The chosen ones that God has put on Earth
To rule the vulgar peasantry and keep
Those riches He decides we ought to reap.
So this, the Dark Caliph's impressive horde,
Should mostly serve myself to help afford
A knightly home, providing for my wife
The trappings of a lord and lady's life.
So therefore I suggest that five percent
To each of you won't make too big a dent
In what's required to house and clothe and feed
My family and meet our every need.'

"On hearing Guy's assertion, Gilbert Black
And Hubert launched a voluble attack
On England's aristocracy of knights
Who trample on the peasants' human rights.
Specific'lly they vilified Sir Guy,
And whilst he was in earshot vowed to die
Ensuring that the just desserts they'd earned
Were given, and declared if Gisborne spurned
Their claims for equal shares there'd come a day
When one way or another he would pay.

"To me, said Gilbert, 'Join our cheerless ranks
To claim your dues, for Gisborne owes us thanks
For risking all against those undead beasts.'

"Yet I replied, 'The wants and needs of priests
Are diff'rent from the wants of common folk.
And though I'm disappointed, let's not soak
Our minds in sops of hatred and revenge
Lest for our sins God chooses to avenge
Himself on us for pilfering this loot.
Instead, let's praise the Lord no ghoulish brute

35

Was able to recruit us to the mob
Of shambling corpses, leaving us the job
Of pocketing the spoils of war that lout
The Dark Caliph concealed in his redoubt.'

"'I know that five percent is but a crumb
Of what we found, but still it's such a sum
In monetary terms to keep one snug
Till years from now one's resting place is dug.'

"These words of mine did little to placate
My comrades though their anger did abate
Enough for them to put their threats on hold—
At least till we unloaded all our gold
And other riches on an English beach.
For in my mind I feared we might not reach
Our homeland if the rough and ready crew
Got wind of what our cargo was and threw
Us overboard to drown beneath the waves
Where Neptune's spacious bed might be our graves.

"I pondered hard this turning of events,
Of Gisborne's greed and of those gaping rents
Now threatening to tear our pact apart
And causing much distress unto my heart.

"So as the night closed in I took a walk
From prow to stern and heard the idle talk
Of crewmen saying once the voyage was done
They'd spend some time with fam'ly or in fun
In taverns drinking beer and picking fights
Before again transporting gallant knights
And pilgrims to the land where Jesus roamed.

"I ceased my aimless sauntering and combed
The sea for signs of ships and foreign coasts.

I turned and spied two figures—vague as ghosts—
Illuminated 'neath the crescent moon,
Stood midst the weary sailors who were strewn
Beneath the lofty fo'c's'le and on deck.

"I heard the lady, Claire, complain her neck
Still troubled her, at which the second shape
Inspected her infected, ruddy nape.
I recognized the second form as Guy,
Who touched her wound, eliciting a cry
Of pain, so I began to softly creep
Between the curled-up crewmen (now asleep)
Until I had an unimpeded view
Of Lady Claire's raw wound of scarlet hue.

"'We'll keep your hurt a secret from the rest,'
Said Gisborne, 'for we've passed the port of Brest
And soon enough will touch on English soil
Where at a skilled physician's hand we'll foil
The poison that is flowing through your veins
And racking you with sundry aches and pains.'

"On hearing this intriguing speech I sought
To recollect the happ'nings at the fort.
This brought to mind the incident I braved
The undead Dark Caliph and smartly saved
Our Lady Claire before our foe could rip
Her throat apart and sup her blood or strip
The organs from her abdomen and chest.

"But now it seemed the lady wasn't blessed
With luck, for from a scratch or through a nick,
The malady of death had done its trick
And worked its way twixt damaged bits of skin
Till finally it found a pathway in."

Chapter IX

"On tiptoe, I returned to my own place
Upon the deck and made myself a space
Beside the archer, Hubert, and our friend,
The soldier Gilbert Black, so they might lend
Their ears to me and talk about our plight
Upon this ship where still the zombie blight
Held sway within the veins of Lady Claire.

"Said Hubert, 'This deceitful, shifty pair
Must make a choice, for Guy's infected wife
Must sacrifice her own ill-fated life
Or have it taken by her loving spouse.
This malady of death we have to douse
Before the lady makes of us a meal
Or gives us this disease that none can heal.'

"The three of us, on this, were all agreed,
Deciding that we had to intercede
Before the grim contagion reached dry land
As Gisborne and his ailing wife had planned.
And so we rose and ventured to confront
This couple ere the lady, Claire, might hunt
For meat amongst the passengers and crew
If in her veins this vile infection grew.

"The noble pair at first denied the claim
Of negligent endangerment—a lame

And sorry refutation since the back
Of Claire's infected neck had now turned black.

"At length, however, Guy confessed the truth.
Said he, 'Let's keep the facts from these uncouth
And wicked-looking crewmen till the deed
To euthanize doth terminate this breed
Of monsters emanating from the East,
Before my lovely Claire becomes a beast.'

"Though hollow-eyed and mottle-skinned the wife
Of Guy placed in her husband's hand a knife.
She urged him to escort her to the bow,
And on the fo'c's'le, high above the prow
Dispatch her with alacrity then hurl
Her corpse into the oceanic swirl.

"So Gilbert Black and Hubert both withdrew
To where they bunked amidships 'mongst the crew,
Whilst to the vessel's stern I fast retired
To pray for Claire until her life expired,
And then to ask our Lord to take her soul
And let it reach its everlasting goal.
Eventu'lly I saw a dagger flash
In moonlight, followed by a heavy splash
And figured that the zombie plague would cease,
Now Lady Claire had gained eternal peace.

"Believing that Sir Guy would need some time
To come to terms with such a grievous crime
As killing one's own wife I knelt in prayer
For hours both for him and Lady Claire.
But then from my devotions I was yanked
By movement and observed that crewmen flanked
My two companions, threat'ning and irate.
And there behind them, faces filled with hate,

Were Gisborne and his living lady spouse.

"It seemed that Guy, the double-dealing louse,
Had fooled us with a brandished blade and sack
Of grain which he discarded in the black
And choppy Channel waters, then he paid
To have my friends (deemed knotty problems) slayed.

"Ere Gilbert Black or Hubert fully woke,
Sir Guy implored the paid-off crew to poke
Their daggers deep inside their victims' flesh
Unto the hilts, until they dripped with fresh
And new-shed blood to stain the deck bright red.

"So that was what was done, and then those dead,
Assassinated fighting men were tossed
Into the sea where quickly they were lost
From sight beneath the waves around Dieppe.

"Before their killers took a further step
I leapt unto my feet and grabbed my sword,
Then in my habit tumbled overboard
And struck out strongly, heading for the coast
Of Normandy whilst hounded by a host
Of crossbow bolts and arrows from that ship
Which carried me upon a luckless trip.

"The boat, however, didn't turn around
Through fear that on a reef 'twould run aground.
Instead, the murd'rous sailors headed east,
Perhaps convinced this problematic priest
Was lying at the bottom of the sea,
To leave their brutal actions witness free."

Chapter X

"Conveyed upon the currents and the tide,
Exhausted, I swam on until I spied
A lantern in the window of a hut,
And though the coastal shingles bruised and cut
My hands and feet, I made my way ashore
And knocked upon the hovel's wooden door.

"The fisherman who lived inside the house
Observed that I was shiv'ring like a mouse
From shock and from fatigue and bitter cold.
And though I offered up the stash of gold
Within my purse, the man just shook his head
And bid me, take for free his modest bed.

"For one whole week I lay twixt life and death,
Affected by a fever whilst my breath
Was labored, causing pain within my chest.
Yet Jean-Pierre—the Frenchman—did his best
To nurse me from the brink and back to health
And saved me from the patient Reaper's stealth.

"In Latin, Jean-Pierre and I conversed,
That common tongue in which we both were versed.
And when he understood the crucial stand
I had to make to stop an undead band
From zombifying England's kith and kin
(By infiltrating through abraded skin

Their strange corruption), naught could halt my friend
From taking me to Dover in the end.

"In Jean-Pierre's small fishing boat we sailed
Across the English Channel, where we hailed
A boy upon the beach who set us right,
Directing us towards those cliffs of white.
We anchored just off shore, in pouring rain,
And since the morning tide was on the wane
I jumped into the water, to my waist
And waded through the waves until I graced
Once more the verdant land where I was born.
''Tis time,' cried I to Jean-Pierre, 'to warn
My countrymen about this plague which might
Consume them all, but since it's not your fight
I urge you to return to France with speed
And pray that on my mission I succeed.'

"My foreign chum, though reticent to leave,
Expressed his hopes I'd speedily achieve
My goal to rid my homeland of this bug.
Then with a thumbs-up gesture and a shrug
He weighed his anchor, turned about and gave
Myself a final, hearty farewell wave.

"With just my ragged clothing and my sword,
And in my velvet purse a modest hoard
Of gold and silver coins to pay my way
I climbed the cliffs till Dover's harbored bay
Was lying in the sun, below my feet.
I clambered down and on a dockside street,
I booked into a hostelry to rest
Ere seeking out the zombie's newfound nest.

"It seemed that Guy and Lady Claire set forth
Five days before to London, heading north.

And then, according to their stated will,
They carried on (since Claire was pale and ill)
To Nottingham—or so my landlord claimed.
For news of trav'lers passing through as famed
As Gisborne and his poorly wife spread fast.

"On hearing these reports I sat aghast
And wondered whether Lady Claire had changed
Into a ghoulish cannibal that ranged
The London streets, in which case all was lost.
If not, I knew no matter what the cost,
I had to put a stop to this disease.

"So once the Lord had heard my desp'rate pleas
For mercy, I secured myself a horse
And saddled her before I set my course
For England's famous capital and found
That on her streets no zombies did abound.
Instead, the news from Nottingham concerned
A highwayman named Robin Hood who'd learned
To prey on those of affluence, then shared
The proceeds with his countrymen who fared
Less well beneath the Normans' brutal boot.

"I realized then that Gisborne's stolen loot
Could act as bait for Robin Hood—a hook
By which I might entice the noble crook.
Yet first to Sherwood Forest's leafy den
(Of Robin and his hundred merry men)
I had to reach before Sir Guy got word
That Friar Tuck, the tough, elusive bird,
Still lived and didn't care for war-won spoils,
But wanted God's assistance in his toils
To end the tainted life of Lady Claire.

"At Ashby-de-la-Zouche's bimonthly fair
I left my horse and carried on by foot.
Then round my neck, upon a cord, I put
This leper's bell to keep those troops away
That help the Sheriff and Sir Guy hold sway
Until I'd scoured this verdant, tree-filled wood
And told my tale to Robin of the Hood."

Chapter XI

A silence had descended on the band
Of outlawed men, as nervously they scanned
The undergrowth and trees for further ghouls
That lurked within the shadows and the pools
Of dappled light which seemingly now held
A host of beasts by thirst for blood compelled
To seek out those alive to meet their need.

Said Robin, "These ungodly creatures feed
On living, human flesh, and as we've seen
And heard from Friar Tuck, one bite will mean
You join the zombie ranks, compelled to kill,
Not worrying whose blood you choose to spill.
'Tis safe to say this malady's now spread
From Claire and swelled the ranks of those undead.
So time has come to formulate a plan
And if you be a brave and fearless man,
Let's go at once unto our secret glade
To strategize and figure how we'll raid
The Sheriff's castle—lair to Guy's sick wife—
Before this outbreak's prevalence is rife."

An atmosphere of hesitance prevailed,
And several outlaws visibly had paled.
Then Tuck stood up, took off his leper's bell
And swapped it for a cross so fiends from Hell
Might keep away whilst giving him the strength

To use his staff and broadsword's bladed length
To put these walking corpses in their tomb,
Encumbering the coming day of doom.

The group of men strode swiftly through the brush,
And forded streams where crystal waters gush.
They followed paths that took them far and deep
Through Sherwood Forest, till they found a steep
Embankment looming high above the head.
Then over this obstruction Robin led
His merry band and gutsy Friar Tuck
Who found a scene to sorely test his pluck
Occurring in the outlaw's secret camp.

Below, the forest floor was stained and damp
With blood, and strewn with limbs and gory hunks
Of meat, whilst fighting o'er these still warm chunks
Were scores of zombies, vying for the cuts
Most flavorsome, or ripping out the guts
From twitching torsos lying on the ground.

The victims whom the undead horde had downed
Were mainly outlaw comrades and their kin,
Whilst those unholy beasts who'd done them in
Consisted both of villagers and troops
From Nottingham, who sat in ghoulish groups
And dined upon the remnants of their prey.

Said Friar Tuck, "For Guy's rash deeds we pay,
Since in his castle quarters his dear wife
Hath seemingly departed from this life
And resurrected from her fatal bed
This strange disease which starts its morbid spread
Amongst the Sheriff's soldiery and those
Poor country folk not quick upon their toes.

Made motionless and dumb by what they saw
(Their minds and bodies shocked unto the core),
The highwaymen looked on as in a dream
Till suddenly they heard a woman scream.

"'Tis Marion!" cried Robin. "By the caves!
And Little John! They're not yet in their graves.
And next to them is Allin-of-the-Dale,
The former minstrel, brandishing a flail.
These caverns are their ultimate retreat,
And if upon our toes we are not fleet,
Their lives will join the numbers of the slain
Or those whose single impulse in the brain
Is urging mastication of a stiff
That's not yet cold, nor putrid to the sniff."

Whilst Robin spoke, the zombies ceased to dine,
And then, as if responding to a sign
They split their forces, sensing pristine meat
To feed their queer, voracious urge to eat.

The smaller group descended on the caves,
Where Little John and Allin wielded staves
To smite the rabid beings till their skulls
Split open like the fragile wooden hulls
Of storm-tossed ships aground upon a reef.

The larger bunch attacked the brigand chief
And outlawed men who stood upon the bank.
With awkward, shambling gait and flesh that stank
Of fetid death, they scrambled up the slope.
Their jaws began to chomp, their hands to grope
On seeing the objectives of their quest.

Said Friar Tuck, "With arrows let's arrest
These creatures, ere their obstinate advance

Should reach its goal. So why not make them dance
With points of steel that penetrate the brain."

And as the beasts closed in, a deadly rain
Of arrows hit their ranks, and if one struck
Above the neck they tumbled through the muck
And dirt until at last they came to rest,
Immobile, like a newly slaughtered pest,
Upon the blood-soaked ground of Robin's dell,
To stir no more from where their bodies fell.

The bandits were outnumbered, so to stop
The zombie hordes before they reached the top
And breasted the embankment with their claws
And teeth prepared for furthering their cause
Did not leave Robin's men too overjoyed.

The outlaws though, with hopefulness, were buoyed
On seeing that these monsters might be slayed.
So with their staffs and swords they deftly laid
About their foes and added to the toll
Strewn dead around the bottom of the knoll.

But casualties on either side occurred
And Robin's men who'd bled to death now stirred
And rose instilled with hunger and with thirst,
Each vying in their zeal to be the first
To taste their erstwhile comrades' blood and gulp
Those fluids pumped through gory, bleeding pulp.

The battle raged till victory was near
For Robin, since those zombies in the rear
When battle started now were at the fore.
Then finally the Fighting Friar swore
An oath to God and massacred the last
Of those abominations that had cast

Their undead selves upon the lofty bank.

"'Tis not a fitting time," said he, "to thank
The mighty Lord for giving us success
Against these foes, for now we must suppress
The foul reanimations at the caves
Before your pals become the Devil's slaves
And mindlessly seek out their former friends
For sustenance, to meet their morbid ends."

Brave Robin had no need for telling twice,
But bounded down the inclined slope to slice
The noggins from the shoulders of the men
Of Nottingham who'd died then lived again.

With Marion's immortal soul at risk,
Her lover, Robin, set about with brisk
And businesslike demeanor to dispatch
The lumb'ring beasts with swordplay till the patch
Of earth around the caves was tainted red
And all his zombie enemies lay dead.

Chapter XII

The fair and lovely Marion embraced
Her paramour whose timeliness and haste
In coming to her aid had kept her soul
And body both immaculate and whole.
The bandit's thanks went out to Little John,
His tall and stocky right-hand man who'd gone
To any lengths to save his master's lass
By fighting off the frenzied zombie mass.
And Allin, too, took credit for the skill
With which his twirling staff was used to kill
Those vile reanimations and defend
A lady from a fearful, gruesome end.

Said Friar Tuck, "A question still remains
Unanswered, which is how these fiends had brains
Enough to find your secret forest camp?
Or was the smell of living folk the lamp
That lit their way and brought them to their food?"

The Friar's pond'rings left a somber mood
Amongst the glade's survivors and their gloom
Grew deeper since they felt the Day of Doom
Was close at hand, till Little John recalled
The hag who'd led the famished fiends and mauled
Their sentries ere the living dead attacked.

"This creature was the first of them I hacked
To bits," said Little John, "before we found
The only way to kill them was to pound
Their heads until the brain inside was mush
And through the splintered skull began to gush.
I fear this monster still might be undead
And lies beneath the piles of stiffs which fed
Upon our ill-starred comrades till you came
To rescue us. Alas that raging dame
Was Much's mum, a woman well aware
Of who lived in our surreptitious lair
And where it was located in the wood."

On hearing this, young Much now understood
His mother had been guide unto the clan
Of beasts which murdered nearly to the man
The followers of Robin and those folk
Who'd cast away the Sheriff's brutal yoke
To find a hidden haven 'mongst the trees—
A place to live not cringing on their knees.

He sprinted to the heaps of those undead
Who'd fallen in the clearing lest they bred
Another generation of their kind,
Then hunted through the carcasses to find
The woman who had lent to him her womb,
Yet now lay sprawled within this gory tomb.

Before he could be stopped, the miller's son
Had spotted movement underneath a ton
Of zombie flesh, then searching for his goal,
Cast some remains aside and made a hole
(An action that was ill-conceived and dumb)
In hopes he might resuscitate his mum.

No sooner had he cleared a man-sized space,
Than Much's mother, wearing on her face
A look of wrath, erupted through the breach,
Her clawing hands endeavoring to reach
Her shell-shocked son to rip his flesh apart,
To tear into his ribs and eat his heart.
But Robin had the drop on her and bent
His longbow and with expertise he sent
An arrow humming through the air that passed
From ear to ear and gave her rest at last.

Said Marion, "This incident we've seen
Played out confirms these zombies have no keen
Or heightened sense of smell, but found this glade
By one whom in this camp some time has stayed.
Her memories were seemingly intact
Enough that with her followers she hacked
A path to this encampment in the trees
To fall on us like clouds of biting fleas."

The import of this data wasn't lost
On Friar Tuck, who said, "At any cost
We must prevent the spread of this disease.
And if we're to succeed then we must tease
These creatures into congregating where
We'll butcher them—no zombie can we spare.
For if this ailment's progress we can't thwart,
Beyond the Sherwood borders twill be caught
And once those fiends have reached the Great North Road
Across the land this sickness will explode.
So if we let infected creatures stray
At will, they could in course discern their way
From Nottingham, and thus the English race
Will disappear without a single trace."

Asked Robin, "What's the plan that you propose?
For if we are to stalwartly oppose
The fury of a raging, zombie swarm
A strategy of battle we must form.
We cannot hole up here amongst the trees,
But must by brave endeavors strive to seize
Control of some impregnable redoubt
Which keeps through its defenses zombies out
Yet by our presence functions as a lure
From which we can dispense a lasting cure
To every undead creature in the shire."

All eyes now turned upon the Fighting Friar,
Who said, "The Sheriff's castle has a bell
Inside the chapel, tolling with a knell
Which surely will attract each rabid beast
From south, from north and from the west and east
To rally at the sturdy fortress gate
Whilst we stand fast behind the door as bait.
Then from the lofty ramparts we'll dispense
A hail of sudden death in Man's defense."

The outlaw chief considered Tuck's design
And said, "To make the Sheriff's castle mine
Is only half the job, for there inside
A host of hungry zombies might reside.
This infestation needs to be wiped out
And since, by nature, English hearts are stout
I have no doubt our goodness shall prevail,
That this infernal plague of death shall fail
To pass beyond our district of our isle
As long as we conduct ourselves with guile.
So let us execute the Friar's plan.
The battlements at Nottingham we'll man
And with the chapel bell attract to us
These fest'ring folk that stink of rot and pus.

They know the castle well, for when alive
This region was the place they used to drive
Their cows and till their meager fields of wheat.
So when they hear our bell, they'll set their feet
Towards our buttressed building where we'll stand
And decimate this blight upon our land."

Chapter XIII

"The journey to the castle will be strewn
With danger such that no one but a loon
Would make the trip," warned Allin-of-the-Dale
As from the trees there came a bunch of pale
And mutilated creatures dressed in rags.
Amongst them there were children, maids and hags
All blood bespattered, hoping for a taste
Of human blood and gathering with haste
Upon a bridge that spanned a running stream.

"They block our route," said Friar Tuck, "and seem
To know that those alive will need to ford
The river at this point, so ask the Lord
For strength to overcome this evil brood
Which want to make you Sherwood men their food."

Without delaying, Robin Hood attacked
These serfs transformed to living dead and hacked
A swathe of carnage through the famished mob.
Then in his wake (and wrapping up the job
Of separating zombies from their heads
Before they might transmit the germ which spreads
From scratches and from bites) were Friar Tuck
And Little John and Allin who'd soon struck
The noggins from the necks of every fiend.
Yet ere upon their sharpened blades they leaned
Exhausted, they discovered that their foes

Had managed with their nails, in the throes
Of death to scratch those outlawed men whose fear
Had put them during battle in the rear.

In total there were three whose legs were hurt
So gravely that infected grime and dirt
Was fast proliferating in their veins.
It racked them with excruciating pains,
Necessitating Friar Tuck to use
His sword before their ruddy, facial hues
Became Death's sickly shade, as gray as ash.

As soon as all had made the dang'rous dash
Across the bridge, avoiding any chance
Of twitching fingers reaching out to lance
And open up the skin around their shins
(Or poking through their fleeing feet like pins),
Maid Marion espied a brace of men
Perambulating in a nearby glen.

The miller's son, young Much, yelled for the pair
To join their band and bravely do their share
To save their fledgling nation from the curse
Of zombies ere the pestilence got worse,
Affecting every corner of the land.

The men drew close and vowed to lend a hand:
The first, dressed in a tunic proved to be
A Forester, whose mandate was to see
The woodland laws enforced, that if a deer
Were poached to fill the populace with fear
By tracking down the killer of the beast
And ruining that serf's unlawful feast.
He'd apprehend the poor, malnourished wretch,
Then amputate the fingers used to stretch
A bow and loose an arrow at its goal.

The second man had murdered quite a toll
On outlawed men; a loathsome tub of lard,
He acted as the Captain of the Guard
For Nottingham's cruel Sheriff and would hang
All those presumed to be in Robin's gang
Without a second thought, nor with regret.

But now, through mutual need, the bandits let
This pair of villains join them on their quest
To decimate the evil zombie pest.
Yet ere the Sherwood brigands and these two
Obnoxious stragglers rallied to renew
Their passage to the castle where they hoped
From safety to destroy these things that loped
Around the English countryside, they tasked
The Captain to explain himself and asked,
"How came this weird disease to get abroad
From Nottingham's stone ramparts, for a horde
Of creatures now exists where once just one
Existed 'neath the life-provoking sun?"

Chapter XIV

The Captain of the Guard sat on a log
And said, "'Twas Guy, the double-dealing dog.
Two weeks ago, when Lady Claire arrived
From Palestine, she barely had survived
The journey, though her death was close at hand.
She couldn't walk, and hardly could she stand.
So Gisborne and my men transferred her to
Guy's quarters in the courtyard where he drew
The bolt behind the door and kept her locked
From sight with any access to her blocked
Except for one physician who was skilled
In medicine, whose cranium was filled
With knowledge of the supernatural arts.

'Upon her neck, she has a wound that smarts,'
The Doctor told me secretly, 'which taints
Her blood and soon will have her with the saints.
Each day the Reaper's shadow closes in
And on her shriveled form a death's-head grin
Doth spread across her gaunt and fleshless face.
Yet strangely, to avoid his wife's embrace
Sir Guy has tied his consort to her bed
Although she's weak and shortly shall be dead.'

"This medico was with her as she died,
And when her faithful husband went outside
To grieve for his lost wife, to cry and mourn,

The maids-in-waiting came about to fawn
Upon the lifeless body which was sprawled
Across the sheets with features that appalled
Their dainty sensibilities and drew
From some of them the sudden urge to spew.
But though she stank like putrefying meat,
They gathered round and freed her hands and feet.
'Twas then, the Doctor told me, that her eyes
Sprung open and to everyone's surprise
She launched herself upon a timid maid
And bit her neck, from which the lifeblood sprayed.

"Sir Guy, who had been wand'ring in a daze,
On hearing screams ran back beneath the gaze
Of guards upon the battlements to warn
That from his wife a devil would be born.
Alas, his intervention was too late,
For Claire's foul shell had managed to create
A half a dozen more voracious ghouls.
Those maids who were unaltered fought through pools
Of viscous gore, effecting their escape,
Avoiding being chewed about the nape
By Guy's reanimated wife or those
Young girls who from untimely death arose.

"The Doctor and these damsels quickly fled,
Though some of them from bites and scratches bled,
Which caused amongst the soldiery much talk
On whether they should kill these maids or baulk
At Guy's command to cut their mortal cord
And put the blameless women to the sword.

"And so the guards debated on the code
Of chivalry, then resolutely stowed
Their weapons for they didn't have the will
To smite a pretty maiden, nor to spill

Her blood upon the cobbled, courtyard floor.
Not even when emerging through the door
Of Gisborne's quarters came the Lady Claire
And all the undead women did they dare
Believe in Guy's insistence that the dead
Were rising up as fiends intent to spread
Their illness, and by doing so to spawn
An army, as unholy beasts reborn.

"The spell upon the guards was broken when
The first of them was slaughtered like a hen
Whose neck upon the chopping block gets thwacked.
On either side a shambling maid attacked
And plunged her chomping teeth into his throat,
Ere worrying the flesh as would a stoat.

"The sentries drew their blades and set to work,
Whilst on the ground their friend began to jerk;
Yet this belated call to arms was not
Enough to kill the ghouls nor stop the rot.
The damsels' gnashing jaws were far too close
And in a blink infused a deadly dose
Of vile disease in those who stood too near,
Whilst guards with opportunity jumped clear.
They fought a rearguard action for their lives,
Dispensing death with broadswords and with knives.
But then they learned the damsels in the rear
(The wounded ones, who'd been engulfed with fear,
Who stood behind the last defensive line)
Were suddenly transformed and keen to dine
Upon those men protecting them from death.

"Hostilities were over in a breath,
The gruesome sirens sharing out the spoils
Of those they'd killed and gnawing on their coils
Of guts, whilst those whose flesh they now consumed,

Reanimated, rose, and then resumed
A life-begot-from-death in search of prey,
Devouring any persons in their way.

"The zombies gained the upper hand, so I
Sought out the able guidance of Sir Guy.
Yet from afar I saw he was undead
And on our butchered soldiery now fed.
'Twas up to me to save those men I could
And order them to run into the wood,
Escaping from the charnel house our fort
Had now become, and though the route was fraught
With danger from the courtyard to the gate,
Myself and several guards put trust in Fate.

"Yet ere we made our dash beyond the walls
Of Nottingham's great castle, several calls
For help were heard, and from the central keep
We saw the Sheriff and his fam'ly peep
Above the tower's battlements and plead
The soldiers to return at once and lead
A rescue, and to prove their hearts were bold.
The Sheriff even offered pots of gold
And silver and of gems for those who stayed,
But those who did as asked were soon waylaid.

"And thus it came to pass that only two
Escaped alive into the trees to rue
The day Sir Guy came back from his crusade.
Myself and Gisborne's doctor quickly made
Our getaway, though trailing in our wake
Were sev'ral of those beasts intent to slake
Their thirst and make us join their evil brood.

"We wandered for a day till want of food
Directed us to Sherwood village, where

I told the Sheriff's forester a rare
And dang'rous germ had made the castle fall
To Satan's cohorts, leaving but a small
Contingent of survivors in the keep,
As well as I, who, much deprived of sleep,
Decided to partake of forty winks
Believing I'd outrun the zombie jinx."

Chapter XV

Because the Captain's tale had now been told
Of how the castle fell, 'twas time to scold
The man on his gross negligence to leave
The gate wide open rather than to cleave
As many zombie skulls as could be split,
Whilst keeping those infected in the pit
Created twixt the buttressed fortress walls.

"You let them roam the countryside that sprawls
Beyond the Sheriff's stony-walled redoubt,"
Charged Much who cuffed the chubby, thoughtless lout
For laxity that caused his mother's end
Instead of fighting bravely to defend
The Sheriff's kin as duty had required.

"In blame and guilt we risk becoming mired,"
The Forester piped up, "so let me tell
The story from the point the Captain fell
Asleep inside my cottage, on my bed.

"Soon after came the zombie masses led
By guards who in these parts had oft patrolled
To ruthlessly enforce each tax the cold
And heartless Sheriff opted to impose.
Their numbers were augmented too by those
Subsiding near the castle, tilling land
And drafted to the gruesome zombie band.

"Yet unprepared were we for their assault.
And this, the crazy Doctor was at fault,
For though the Captain's story had induced
Conviction, this belief was fast reduced
By Gisborne's own physician's rants and raves
Of creatures resurrected from their graves.
With bulging eyes and flailing arms he told
The villagers of hellish fiends that doled
Out certain death with tooth and sharpened claw,
Then feasted on their victims' flesh and gore.

"And while the serfs and peasantry guffawed,
A warning voice cried out and said, 'A horde
Of those possessed by Satan fast approach
The village and already do encroach
Upon our fields with awkward, shambling gait,
Whilst by our houses more of them await.'

"We looked around and found these words were true.
About us was a deadly noose that drew
Much tighter with each second we delayed.
The zombies ringed the village and they preyed
On anyone who tried to get away,
Till mutilated, limbless corpses lay
About the fields and hovels, where a poor
Community once stood but stood no more.

"As one by one the village folk succumbed,
I watched and quaked, my mind and body numbed.
Then as the shuffling specters gathered round,
The Doctor made a frightened, bleating sound
Which broke the spell and reaffirmed my wits.
So as the zombies grabbed and tore to bits
The whimpering physician, I made haste
And sprinted to my home, though I was chased

By half a dozen zombies whom I locked
Outside the cottage door, which soon I blocked
With furniture to keep the fiends held back.
But oh, my future suddenly looked black.

"Then cow'ring in the corner like a child,
In hopes his body wouldn't be defiled
By agents of the Reaper I perceived
The Captain of the Guard; and feeling peeved
I urged him, 'Stand your ground and be a man!
Let's formulate between ourselves a plan
By which we might escape,' and thus we made
An op'ning in the roof, for if we stayed
Inside my cottage, ultimately these
Reanimated monsters would appease
Their appetites upon our yielding flesh.

"So speedily we took apart the mesh
Of thatching, and evaded just in time
The clutching hands of zombies, for our climb
Onto the roof concluded as the door
Gave way and toppled, crashing to the floor.

"Outside, the undead legions had devoured
The villagers and now they searched and scoured
The hovels for survivors, so we leapt
From roof to ground, then quietly we stepped
Unseen into the woods, and ere espied
Were safely in the trees, with Death defied.

"And that, my friends," the Forester declared,
"Is how we got away and why we fared
Much better than the Sherwood village folk
Whose destiny was seemingly to soak
With blood the earth around their humble huts,
Whilst having monsters gnawing at their guts."

Chapter XVI

Said Robin to his men, "From what we're told
The Sheriff's with his fam'ly and his gold
Inside the keep, and if the door is strong
Those few remaining zombies won't stay long
But search the nearby neighborhood for meat
That's easier to capture, kill and eat.
So let's continue trudging to the fort
Of Nottingham before this wood is fraught
With danger from these roaming zombie bands
That zealously depopulate our lands."

The woods and glades of Sherwood were devoid
Of humans, like a lifeless, untamed void,
And through the trees the living men travailed.
Not once were they endangered or assailed
Until they reached a brook whose shallow flanks
Were overlooked by grassy, blood-stained banks.
Yet since the stream was strewn with hefty stones
To step upon, preventing trav'lers' bones
From getting chilled, the Captain of the Guard
And Forester were happy to discard
Both vigilance and caution and to cross
At this ill-omened spot or face a loss
Of time in seeking out another site
To ford before the coming of the night.

So off they rushed, while Robin tried to guess
The meaning of the red, discolored mess
That dyed the grass as if some ghouls had laid
Quite recently a crafty ambuscade.

Upon the stepping stones the two men trod
Whilst Friar Tuck prepared his wooden rod
In case a sly deception was in play.
Then ere the foolish pair had gone half way,
The water round the rocks began to churn
And though they tried upon their heels to turn,
From deeper regions in the stream emerged
The shapes of sev'ral monsters that converged
Upon the two unwary men, then hauled
Them screaming from the stepping stones and mauled
Their necks until the river flowed bright red.
And whilst upon their fleshy limbs they fed,
The Friar, with his quarterstaff jumped in
The running brook (unruffled by the din
The dying men were making) and let fly
A blow that caught a zombie in the eye
And penetrated to its rotten brain.
He followed this maneuver with a rain
Of well-aimed strikes which crushed to pulp the heads
Of three more fiends and cut what mortal threads
Were keeping them from lying in their grave
As single-minded, raging beasts that crave
The pulsing flesh of those not yet diseased.

The fight was touch-and-go till Robin eased
The odds when from his bow he launched a raft
Of arrows making certain every shaft
Transfixed its goal until the fatal ruck
Had only one survivor—Friar Tuck.

Cried Robin, as he lent that man a hand
And pulled him from the brook to solid land,
"Thou art the strangest monk I've ever known.
Though plump you fight as if your wits have flown—
Without restraint—which causes me to ask
What motivation makes you take to task
These wicked fiends that cheated Death and eat
A person from his head down to his feet?"

So as the robber band traversed the stones
Across the brook whilst list'ning out for moans
From zombies that perchance might be in wait
For easy meat, the Friar told him straight:
"I spoke to you of treasures which were brought
From Palestine and lie inside the fort
At Nottingham; well this must be the gold
And other loot the evil Sheriff told
His guards he'd share if only they'd protect
His family from those who might infect
The ones he loves with zombie-making plague.

"But how he gained Guy's plunder, this is vague,
Unless Sir Guy required his spoils secure
Inside his uncle's keep so not to lure
His men into temptation if the wealth
Was left inside his rooms where Claire's ill health
Was causing much distraction and concern.

"This treasure is the prize I hope to earn
By fighting like a devil, then the poor
Might share this pilfered bounty. So before
The Sheriff uses stolen loot to buy
That place where faith and loyalty should lie
Within the hearts of noblemen and those
Capricious men of cloth whose ebbs and flows
Of constancy depends upon their purse,

I'll grant them first privation's abject curse.
For if the Sheriff sends this treasure on
To purchase their allegiance to Prince John,
The peasants, serfs and other Saxon folk
Will die beneath that tyrant's regal yoke.
'Tis better that this money go to feed
The people in this country most in need."

The openhanded thief was mighty pleased
And told the chubby Friar, "Once we've seized
The castle, then the Sheriff's loot is yours
To propagate your philanthropic cause.
But first of all the countryside we'll clear
Of these unholy beasts, both far and near,
By luring them as tasty human bait
And trusting to the fickleness of Fate.
So let's make haste, pick up your slothful pace,
Against the quickly setting sun we race."

Chapter XVII

At twilight, Robin exited the trees
And from the nearby castle heard the pleas
For rescue that the Sheriff and his spouse
Were making from the confines of their house,
That central tower, circled by its dense
And crenellated outer wall defense.
From high inside the keep, the Sheriff called
For help whilst at his side, his lady bawled
Until they saw the people they were keen
To rescue them were dressed in Lincoln green.

"Let's hasten to the Sheriff's lair," said Tuck,
"Across the open grass before our luck
Is changed." But as he said these words a groan
Erupted from close by, then hands held prone
The miller's son, the young, unworldly Much
Who found himself abruptly in the clutch
Of lurking fiends who'd grabbed him by the coat
And on the ground with teeth tore out his throat.

"We cannot save the boy," said Little John,
"And neither can we stay; so let's be gone
As quickly as we can unto the fort
Whilst these reanimations have their sport."

And so the brigands made a headlong dash
Towards the castle, lest there be a clash

Beside the woods or in the open ground.
Yet as they sprinted, Robin turned around
Each dozen steps and let an arrow loose,
Their wooden shafts as fatal as a noose
Would be upon a living, breathing man.
These missiles were so accurate the span
Of twenty beasts he skillfully cut short
Before his band attained the Sheriff's fort.

The open gate, by heads on spikes was flanked,
Though some of them had from their mounts been yanked
By zombies keen to eat the eyes and drain
Each wormy skull's decaying, slimy brain.

Upon arrival, Robin put a guard
On all four towers, then the gate was barred
By Little John, who used a solid plank.
While this occurred the Friar sat and drank
A bowl of beer decanted from a flask
To fan his zeal and keep him up to task.
And in the meantime, Marion sought out
The kitchen where she made a meal for stout
And gallant-hearted Englishmen who fought
This evil which from foreign climes was brought.
And in the central keep, the Sheriff whined
About these rude intrusions, for his mind
Was set on staying put to save his loot
From Robin (whom he deemed a Saxon brute),
Instead of how his fam'ly might survive
The zombies and escape the fort alive.

Yet once the castle grounds were made secure,
'Twas time to bait the zombie-tempting lure.
So once the owls awoke as darkness fell,
The tolling of the chapel's mighty bell
Resounded as the Friar held on tight

Unto the rope and filled the pitch black night
With such a loud, uncompromising knell
It drew to him those monstrous beasts from Hell.

"Fear not!" said Robin Hood, as all about
Their sturdy, unassailable redoubt
A multitude of soulless zombies swarmed.
"By these foul fiends the castle can't be stormed.
They lack the mind and wherewithal to fight
With catapults or rams, nor scale the height
Of battlements with ladders, so let's rest
And on the morrow do to death this pest."

Though many men lay down to grab what sleep
Was feasible considering a heap
Of zombies milled about outside, those men
Most close to Robin fortified their den.
Ere Friar Tuck, the fearless fighting monk
Retired to the comfort of his bunk,
He set up fires and heated vats of oil,
Whilst Little John and Allin chose to toil
Inside the castle armory and found
That arrows in profusion did abound.
These fatal darts they bundled up and placed
Upon the ramparts, so when next they faced
The zombies in the morning all was set
To snare them in a metaphoric net.
And Marion, the maid, was busy, too.
She rigged a winch by which the Sheriff drew
A basket full of victuals for his kin
(Ere famishment should make them frail and thin)
Unto his lofty hideout in the keep,
Above that place his men were killed like sheep.

Throughout the night the philanthropic chief
Of Sherwood's thieves toiled hard to promise grief

To Nottingham's reanimated throng,
Directing his lieutenants though the pong
Emitted by the rotting mob outside
Was difficult for stomachs to abide.

Chapter XVIII

Then finally, when morning broke next day
The living dead extended all the way
From castle wall to distant forest trees.
Said Friar Tuck, descending to his knees,
"Let's pray for those of us today who'll meet
The Reaper and for fortitude to beat
These hungry beasts awaiting human fare."
And with these words he spoke a hopeful prayer.
"Though in Death's shadow fearlessly I walk,
Of failure and of dread I'll never talk,
For in my hands I hold my sword and rod
Whilst in my heart lies strength bequeathed by God."

"Amen!" the merry men intoned, then strung
Their bows whilst once again the bell was rung
Within the chapel, drawing to the fore
The shire's undead hosts for full-blown war.

Said Robin to his archers, "Lucky shots
We'll leave to those colonial Norman clots
Who struck King Harold's orbit with a fluke.
So let each shaft dispatch an evil spook."

The bowmen notched their arrows and took aim,
Then fired their darts to terminally maim
Their targets with a head shot meant to hush
Their groaning and transform their brains to mush.

With sheaves of feathered arrows, true and straight,
The outlaws gave each beast they hit a date
With destiny by making every shot
They made locate the fiend's Achilles spot.
From crenellated battlements they loosed
A flurry of destructive barbs that juiced
The brains in zombies' craniums until
Some hundreds lay upon the ground stock still.

Yet finally the arrows were expired,
And once the last—through Much's skull—was fired,
It seemed that in the ranks of creatures bent
On eating fellow humans quite a rent
Had been created, giving Robin pause
To cheer his men with heartening applause.

Then whilst the Friar heated up the oil
And brought the viscous liquid to the boil,
Both Little John and Allin handed out
The castle's crossbows, aiming for a bout
Of mayhem which would furthermore reduce
The zombie pack with every bolt let loose.
These missiles flew from loopholes in the walls,
Consigning sundry monsters to the halls
Of Hades in a spurt of brains and blood
That left them downed and twitching in the mud.

But all the ammunition soon was spent,
And though the outlaws made an ample dent
In zombie numbers, still they had to lure
The monsters to the gatehouse then procure
A means by which more beasts might be destroyed.
So while the men with victory were buoyed,
They gathered where the ramparts jutted out
Above the gate, then raised a mighty shout
From where their point of vantage overlooked

The undead host, who now, like fish well-hooked,
Had congregated round the wooden door
To scratch and pound its surface ere the floor
About their feet was swallowed up by flame.

For now the opportunity to maim
The zombies was transferred to Friar Tuck
Who said, "Let's fetch the boiling oil and chuck
The scalding liquid down upon their heads,
Ignite it, then we'll snip their mortal threads."

The monsters pressed against the castle gate,
Until it groaned beneath their hefty weight.
Then Friar Tuck and Robin's men retrieved
A cauldron filled with oil and relieved
Its contents on the heads of those below,
Eliciting such cries as brought a glow
Of triumph to each sturdy Saxon heart.
And next, to make a conflagration start,
The holy Friar grabbed a lighted torch
And threw it on the mad mêlée to scorch
The creatures caught beneath the searing rain,
To bake inside their skulls each tainted brain.
A fire of intensity arose,
Accompanied by squeals of pain that froze
The blood inside each breathing person's veins,
Though adding to the humans' deadly gains.

About the gate the zombies' clothing blazed,
Till those aflame flailed uselessly like crazed,
Unruly windmills fuelled by a squall.
Some victims blindly bounced against the wall
Whilst others turned about and screeched out loud
Ere fleeing through the jam-packed ghoulish crowd.

And so the fire spread amongst the hosts
Of ravenous, reanimated ghosts.
The peasant women's woolen gowns and skirts
Erupted 'mongst the throng in fiery spurts,
Whilst undead friars' habits spread their smoke
And fatal flames to tunic, shirt and cloak
Of soldier, serf and zombie child till more
Than half the undead horde had found a door
To agonizing death upon the plain,
To lie there charred and smoldering and slain.

"My brothers from the abbey who oppressed
Their flocks," said Friar Tuck, "and only blessed
Those folk with coins enough to sate their greed
Are paying for their every crooked deed.
They liked too much the pleasures of this world,
And into Hell's grim portal find they're hurled."

On this the outlaws fervently concurred
And by the deaths of Norman troops were stirred
To feel the retribution meted out
Was just, although they harbored earnest doubt
That peasantry deserved this zombie blight
Which changed them into fiends that claw and bite.

Chapter XIX

Yet this was not a time to hold debate
Upon the machinations played by Fate.
For murmurings amidst the zombie swarm
Remaining indicated that the warm
And yielding flesh of living men they craved
Was balanced by the casualties they'd braved.

No more were these reanimations keen
Beneath the deadly ramparts to be seen.
They wavered, seeming disinclined to stay
Like sitting ducks to burn like bone-dry hay.

Said Robin, "These embodiments are bored
Of waiting here for flesh that's yet un-gnawed.
They hung around the Sheriff's keep before,
Eventu'lly abandoning his door
Because they couldn't find a way inside.
So though these beasts are patient and will bide
Their time, they won't remain forever here,
But might invade the countryside, I fear.
This must be stopped, no matter what the cost,
Or else these isles of England will be lost.
So this is my suggestion to conclude
The zombie menace ere that some elude
Our clutches and disseminate their pox:
Unbar the gate, I say, and as a fox
Into the castle grounds we shall entice

Most cunningly these fiends although the price
We pay in life and limb might be quite great.

"But first, before we open up the gate,
With bludgeons and with blades we must prepare
This trap in which we'll artfully ensnare
Our enemies, so let's retire and raid
The armory for weapons that are made
To smash and slice and hopefully curtail
These beasts—and may God help us if we fail."

Thus Robin and his trusted men dispensed
The weaponry required to fight against
Their decimated foe in hand-to-hand
Engagements to destroy the zombie band.
Then drowning out the Sheriff's angry shouts
Accusing Robin's men of being louts
By threatening the safety of his kin,
The Friar, from the chapel, raised a din.
Upon the belfry's sturdy rope he swung,
And once the resonating bell had rung
A dozen times the undead gathered round
The castle gate and then commenced to pound.

This thumping was for Little John a sign
To let the zombies in, then hold the line
Against the flesh-addicted beasts' stampede,
To keep them off before they got to feed
Upon his flesh with nothing but a pole
Of finest oak to save from Hell his soul.

So once the burly man removed the plank
That barred the door, he faced the forward rank
Of mad-eyed zombies, chomping at the bit.
Yet standing fast within the courtyard's pit
He braced himself against their crazed attack

And fought the urge to run and turn his back.

A moment's hesitation, then the horde
Of zombies flooded through the gate and roared
In exaltation seeing fresh, warm meat—
Impatient for the chance to kill and eat.
But as they neared their prey and quickly filled
The castle grounds and in the courtyard milled,
Preoccupation with their quarry's throat
Prevented them to know a tethered goat.

So as the creatures closed upon their man,
The highwaymen enacted Robin's plan.
From every wall a boiling-oil cascade
Announced an unimagined ambuscade.
Those zombies caught beneath the scalding oil
Collapsed in pain as brains began to broil
Within their bony husks, till quite a few
Had tissues in their skulls transformed to stew.

With many beasts enduringly deceased
And total numbers critically decreased,
'Twas time for single combat: one-on-one.
From all four towers men were seen to run
With bludgeons (flail, or quarterstaff, or mace),
Or blades of sharpened steel with which to face
The remnants of this decimated mob
That wanted through desire for flesh to rob
The living of their will so they might stalk
Our land where feet of Saxon heroes walk.

Chapter XX

Surprise was on the Sherwood bandits' side
And dozens of the zombie pack had died
Before the grim abominations knew
That Robin and survivors from his crew
Were hid about the castle ere their chance
Arrived to make these dreaded monsters dance.

With broadsword brandished high, plump Friar Tuck
Attacked the beasts and with momentum struck
Into their mass, with slashes left and right,
To cut a route through which his blade might smite
As many as he could before he fell
Beneath the weight of denizens from Hell.
He sliced through flesh-gorged bellies, spilling guts,
And with his higher, swirling, sweeping cuts
Beheaded those foul creatures in his way
Till one specific smiting made his day.
The Abbott of St. Mary's now appeared
And joyfully the Fighting Friar speared
The glutton, then relieved him of his head
And thanked the Lord this evil man was dead
Who'd sent him on that ill-begot crusade
Where blameless folk were tortured, hanged and flayed.

And meanwhile, stalwart Allin-of-the-Dale
Beset the fiends around him with a flail
That bust the skulls wide open of his foes

And left them in their last convulsing throes.
He made a path until he came upon
His much beleaguered comrade, Little John,
Whose antics with a twirling, oaken cane
Had crushed to pulp each noxious zombie brain
Its length was brought in contact with until
He stood atop a corpse-constructed hill.
And so the friends fought on till Allin felt
An undead maiden grab him by the belt.
She pulled him from the gore-bespattered mound,
Where strugg'ling for his life upon the ground
His body was immobilized by hands
Which soon plucked out his guts in glist'ning strands.

His eyes bedewed with tears, brave Little John
Made certain that his loyal chum had gone
To God Almighty's cradle and caved in
His skull before his carcass might begin
To jerk and be reanimated by
This ailment which precluded men to die.

But what of Robin Hood, the robber chief?
With dagger and with mace he doled out grief
Whilst Marion stood boldly at his side,
Equipped with thrusting sword, a blushing bride
Whose face was splashed with zombies' spurting blood.
They fought as one to stem the vicious flood
Of creatures armed with chomping, gory maws
And kept at bay their grasping, scratching claws.
Yet while they battled on, they saw a face
Well known to them, so Robin swung his mace
With all his might and brought the weapon down
Upon Sir Guy of Gisborne's naked crown.
As blood befouled with brains began to squirt
From Gisborne's head and sully Robin's shirt,
Maid Marion identified a cloak

Amongst the throng of raging, undead folk
Belonging to a man of means whose skills
Involved dispensing drugs and healing pills.
Such livery apothecaries wore,
So with a maiden's meek, rebellious roar
Brave Marion struck off the Doctor's head,
And Guy's physician stood there with a red
Arterial fountain gushing from his neck
Till finally he crumpled to the deck.

Yet even though the zombie masses bore
A dreadful toll, the hero outlaws saw
Their ranks depleted man-by-man until
But few of them remained with blood to spill.

"Unto the keep!" cried Robin. "Let's retreat
To safety ere these apparitions beat
The remnants of our army and enroll
Our valiant survivors in their goal
Of searching out a tender, gory treat,
Of feeding their compulsive need for meat."

Chapter XXI

So Marion, and Little John, and Tuck
(Along with Robin Hood) rode out their luck,
Withdrawing till beside the tower wall
They stood to carry on the desp'rate brawl.
They made their way by inches to the door
Where Little John forced entry when he tore
The structure from its hinges and its bolt.

The Sheriff called down angrily, "You dolt!
You've led these hungry monsters to my rooms
Not caring that your slapdash action dooms
My wife and kids to death unless we stay
Locked up until these zombies go away.
So don't expect my help, my door is barred,
Which means your only haven is the yard
Or other chambers in this keep to save
Your carcasses and shield you from the grave."

Ignoring what the Sheriff said, the four
Surviving Sherwood stalwarts shored the door
With furniture, impeding those without
From entering the fortified redoubt.
Yet obstinately tens of zombies gripped
The heavy door, then pulled until it slipped
From Robin and his staunch supporters' grasp.
The brave quartet let out a fretful gasp,
For nothing stood twixt them and sundry beasts

But benches, chairs and tables used at feasts
And pilfered from the keep's great hall to dam
The zombies' forward progress through the jamb.

The monsters tore apart the barricade
Of furniture, then ran the failed blockade.
This sudden rush of flesh-addicted ghouls
Was met with thrusts and strikes from hostile tools.
With sword and dagger, wooden staff and mace
The final Sherwood four defended space
Inside the keep 'gainst those who'd once been maids,
Or farming folk, or girls with pretty braids.
They also fought tenacious, wild-eyed boys
Who days before had played with children's toys,
And soldiers, tradesmen, nuns and priests and monks
Intent on tearing humans into chunks
Of squishy flesh, then chewing on their bones
To thus assuage their empty-bellied moans.

The zombies pushed a path between their prey
Compelling Little John to back away
Towards those darker regions of the keep—
The dungeons where the Sheriff used to reap
Confessions from his foes, and once they'd sung
In front of thronging crowds he'd have them hung.
So Little John retreated underground
Along a spiral staircase where he found
The cells all locked and not one place to hide
From creatures hoping keenly to divide
The brawny giant's choicest cuts of meat
Unless Death's scythe he cunningly could cheat.

"Alas," said Robin Hood, "our friend is gone,
And lest we share the fate of Little John,
Let's fight a rearguard action and ascend
This staircase leading upwards and defend

The open space within the banquet hall
Before our backs are truly to the wall."

Thus Marion and Tuck—the fighting monk—
Ascended with their leader ere they sunk
Beneath the undead masses at the stairs.
Then from the hall they tossed down stools and chairs
Upon the zombies' heads till they ran out
Of furniture to chuck and throw about.

Resigned to death, and standing back-to-back,
The three survivors battled on to hack
The necks or smash the brains of hungry ghosts
That soon might spread their ailment to the coasts
Of England and perhaps to foreign lands,
Afflicting them with roaming zombie bands.

But then, whilst blades of sharpened metal slashed,
And bludgeons into undead noggins crashed,
A burly figure reached the topmost stair
With quarterstaff in hand and showed his flair
At breaking heads and piercing with his pole's
Blunt ends a zombie's orbits, making holes
That turned the creature's brains to pasty mush.

"'Tis Little John!" cried Tuck and felt the flush
Of victory was hanging in the air;
For by the very thickness of a hair
Had Robin's right hand man evaded those
Who hoped to eat him, helpless, in repose.
But Little John had stood his ground and fought
'Gainst overwhelming odds until he'd taught
The zombies that an Englishman's resolve
Could any supernatural problem solve.

So Sherwood's four brave champions finished off
The last few fiends who'd hoped so much to scoff
The yielding, blood-gorged tissues of a prey
Turned predator till zombie corpses lay
Unmoving and dismembered on the floor
Amidst a slick of fast congealing gore.

Well chuffed were those surviving this mêlée,
Who'd lived through Hell to fight another day.

Chapter XXII

Yet whilst their celebrations carried on,
Above the hall the Sheriff's wife felt wan
And visited her privy, where a bowl
Of water stood beside the cesspit hole.
And while she splashed her face to tame her fear
A scraping sound was captured by her ear.
The noise originated from the chute
Conveying human waste along the route
Directly to the pool of cess below.
She looked into the hole, where oft a glow
Of sunlight showed around the funnel's base.
Yet all was dark, and as she put her face
Much closer to that black, foreboding maw,
Two hands shot out and nails commenced to claw
Her nose and cheeks, then scratched out both her eyes.
The Sheriff's kin were taken by surprise,
For Lady Claire had scaled the filthy pipe
And loitered in the shaft till time was ripe
To spring her trap and violently to stun
Her quarry ere her human prey could run.

The Sheriff's wife pulled free and stumbled out
Into the main apartments with a shout
Of agony which echoed round the keep.
Then Lady Claire came crawling from that steep
And foully coated chimney with a roar.
Before the Sheriff's kids could reach the door

She grabbed the boy and girl and picked them up
In one hand each, and bit their necks to sup
Upon their flesh and spurting scarlet gouts,
Whilst screams of pain drowned out their father's shouts.

This chaos brought the sound of running feet
Upon the stairs, and Robin's men as fleet
As deer approached the studded door of oak
Which John applied his shoulder to and broke.

No sooner was the entrance breached than Claire,
With rabid, staring eyes and flying hair
Ran screaming at this interloping band.
Yet in a jiffy, Robin had in hand
His dagger which he thrust from 'neath her chin
And upwards, that the deadly weapon's thin
And steely blade could penetrate her brain
So from her corpse the undead force would drain.

Yet worse was still to come, and Friar Tuck
Was first to spot the Sheriff's little buck
(A boy of five or six) and pretty lass
Whose fingers delved with gusto in the mass
Of blood and flesh that once had been their dad.
They giggled as they ate and rolled their mad
Unfocused eyes, then dipped their hands and spooned
The entrails from their father's open wound.

Without a second thought the Friar swung
His sword, and with two swipes the heads were flung
Off either sibling 'gainst the chamber walls.
They rolled across the floor like bladdered balls
And came to rest with lolling tongues, and lips
As white as snow and leaking bloody drips.

Though disemboweled, the Sheriff's body stirred
And from his throat a moaning sound was heard.
And as he tried to stagger to his feet,
Heroic Little John punched out a neat
Concentric void, by swiping with his pole
Of oak to make a brain-destroying hole.

Yet what a tragic sight the Sheriff's wife
Provided, for it looked as if a knife
Had scraped away her face and plucked her eyes
From either socket, forcing plaintive cries
Of anguish from her throat that wrung the hearts
Of those who'd played their zombie-killing parts.

But still the nightmare wasn't at an end.
For Robin Hood's compassion made him lend
A hand to help this victim who'd been maimed.
Yet suddenly the woman cruelly tamed
By Lady Claire's attack became a brute,
And though her grievous wounds had made her mute
The zombie pox was flowing through her veins
And urging her to eat the pulsing brains
Of Robin Hood, who stood within her reach.

She locked her teeth on Robin, like a leech,
And bit down hard upon his hatless head.
But ere the creature rendered Robin dead
The bandit chief had swung his hefty mace
And battered in the undead lady's face.
He smashed the skull and crushed the woman's spine,
Which left her twitching on the ground, supine.
Then Marion beheaded with her sword
The Sheriff's wife and cut the spinal cord.

"I'm done," said Robin, "lead me to a bed,
"And do your duty: cut my mortal thread.

But first I beg you, fetch for me a bow
And arrow, and where're the shaft should go,
That place shall be my grave and where I'm lain.
So help me now, before my mortal pain
Should end and leave me seemingly deceased
To come back moments later as a beast."

With heavy hearts both Little John and Tuck
Retreated from the keep to seek and pluck
An arrow from a zombie done to death
Beyond the castle walls. Then as the breath
Was failing in brave Robin's noble chest
They handed him the missile and the best,
Most supple bow discovered near that field
Where many zombies' destinies were sealed.

Though strength was failing, Robin notched the dart
And loosed it through a casement ere his heart
Gave out and left Maid Marion in tears,
Entrusted to belay her lover's fears.
She severed Robin's head as asked, then sobbed
For England's ranks of heroes had been robbed.

Chapter XXIII

The outlaw's corpse was carried in a cart
To where he'd shot his final feathered dart.
And there the Friar, Tuck, and Little John
Dug out a grave, and while the sun still shone
Interred their friend beneath an oak's green leaves—
Good Robin Hood, the noble Prince of Thieves.

Whilst Marion was grieving for her groom,
The two remaining men explored the room
In which the Sheriff's family had died
And found Guy's plundered treasure stuffed inside
A treasure chest which soon lay in the cart
They'd commandeered. But ere they had the heart
To leave that place where many friends and foes
Lay strewn upon the ground to feed the crows,
They piled the corpses up into a pyre
And using boiling oil to stoke the fire
They lit a conflagration which consumed
Those hundreds whom the hand of Death had doomed.

Chapter XXIV

For Marian her future was devoid
Of happiness, for Robin was a void
That weighed upon her heart and dimmed her sun.
Because of this she soon became a nun
At Kirkley, at the priory, whilst Tuck
And Little John in Sherwood Forest struck
A deal to live as hermits in the wood.
They used Sir Guy of Gisborne's loot for good,
And Little John, each year, set out abroad,
Distributing a portion of their hoard.

And even though King Richard made it back
From Palestine, he died in an attack
In Brittany which left Prince John to sit
Upon the throne—a useless, greedy twit.
Alas, the Saxons' lot was not improved
Once Richard, by Death's hand, had been removed.

So, disillusioned, Tuck put on his bell
To ward off folk and sat within his cell
In solitude till he and Little John
From earthly care and agedness were gone.

Epilogue to the Monk's Second Tale

The hour when the tale was done was late,
So fostered little studious debate.
But of one mind, the pilgrims all agreed
'Twas good that England's holts and heaths were freed
Of this exotic menace from the East
When Robin's men destroyed the lowering Beast
That threatened—if this tale be true—the lands
Belonging to Britannic sovereigns' hands.
And though the scary content of this tale
Made many gape and others quake and quail
Most heartily the pilgrims went to bed
And dreamt of England's proud, heroic dead.

Here Endeth the Monk's Second Tale

HORRID HAIKUS

Horrid Haiku One

When facing werewolves
Forget about gems or gold.
Silver's more precious.

Horrid Haiku Two

To put off vampires
Each night eat your evening meal
With much garlic bread.

Horrid Haiku Three

When Freddie threatens
Dream that he's a wimpy nerd
With butterfingers.

Horrid Haiku Four

Friday the thirteenth.
A day to steer well clear of
Hockey stadiums.

Horrid Haiku Five

Stick out both your arms.
Make moaning sounds. Hope zombies
Don't notice a pulse.

Horrid Haiku Six

In America
Werewolves beware! Lone Ranger's
Bullets are silver.

Horrid Haiku Seven

If mummies rampage,
Stand still. They won't notice you
For their bandages.

Horrid Haiku Eight

Hairdressers beware!
Old harridans take off hats—
You transform to stone.

Horrid Haiku Nine

A good almanac's
A vampire's friend. It predicts
Solar eclipses.

Horrid Haiku Ten

Recall *Alien?*
The beast was lucky John Hurt
Didn't like curry.

About the Author

Paul A. Freeman is the author of *Rumours of Ophir*, a crime novel set in Zimbabwe, which is currently on that country's English Literature syllabus. He writes mainly narrative poetry, horror and crime fiction and the first novel in his *Maddox* trilogy (a crime story set in Saudi Arabia) will be published in German translation in 2010. He works as a teaching advisor in Abu Dhabi, where he lives with his wife and three children.

Science. Research. Knowledge. The human intellect knows no bounds because of them. Sometimes . . . science goes wrong.

Death. Destruction. Zombies. Featuring the terrifying tales of 13 authors, *Dead Science* brings you stories of the undead unlike any you've ever read before.

Times are tough. The dead have risen up to feast on the living. Zora, an army deserter who hears voices from above, joins up with a badly scalded nuke-survivor named Zeno in order to locate Ahura Mazda and deliver a taste of justice to the cowards who orchestrated the apocalypse . . . preferably without being served up as zombie lunch-meat.

Zombifrieze: Barnacles

Chev Worke thought he had found a path to easy money. He just didn't count on things going wrong and getting stranded on State Highway 59 with no one around except for a pack of hungry werewolves. Chev makes it to a grocery store in Easter Glen only to learn of a secret pact that has been in place for centuries. There's just one problem: the pact has been broken.

Two mob families go to war and the current Don is buried alive on a construction site that was once the location of a church that had banned the same Don's ancestors. Major problems arise when a group of mysterious Sicilians arrive and manage to retrieve the Don's corpse. Well, his *living* corpse. Before long, the Don's undead state leads to the outbreak of reanimated dead. Capisce? *Don of the Dead.*

The invasion begins and the dead start to rise. There's panic in the streets of London as invaders from Mars wreak havoc on the living. But that's not the only struggle mankind must face. The dead are rising from their graves with an insatiable hunger for human flesh. It's kill or be killed, otherwise you might become one of the walking dead yourself.

The War of the Worlds Plus Blood, Guts and Zombies

This ain't your grandfather's Huckleberry Finn. A mutant strain of tuberculosis is bringing its victims back from the dead. In this revised take on history and classic literature, the modern age is ending before it ever begins. Huckleberry Finn will inherit a world of horror and death, and he knows the mighty Mississippi might be the only way out . . .

Adventures of Huckleberry Finn and Zombie Jim

At Verlaine High, classes are cut short by news of explosions across the river, part of a series of horrific terrorist attacks that paralyze the nation. But that is only the beginning: amber clouds fill the sky, burning rain pelts down, and the surviving students learn that their tormentors have mutated into something far worse—reanimated corpses with a primordial instinct for murder. *The Lifeless.*

In the last days of World War II, an unknown force returns the dead to life. As a new war between the dead and the living rages on, three men hold the key to defeating them. Will they be up to the task before all of Germany and the world fall to the hungry teeth of the undead?

World War of the Dead.

The dead rise. The world dies. Mankind falls and enters Death's halls. Over 90 poems of carnage, hopelessness and despair mixed with oodles of the living dead await you. *Vicious Verses and Reanimated Rhymes: Zany Zombie Poetry for the Undead Head* will not only melt your brain . . . it'll tear out your jugular!

The Wicked Witch of the East has cast a spell on the Land of Oz, a spell that brings the dead back to life. Only the Great Wizard in the Emerald City can stop this curse. It's up to Dorothy, Toto, the Scarecrow, the Cowardly Lion and the Tin Woodman to journey through this land of hungry undead and savage monsters and find him in the hopes of bringing life back to Oz. *The Undead World of Oz.*

After stumbling upon an ancient spell book hidden in the school library, Shawn and Barry decide to get revenge on the school's bully, Mitch Johnson. First stop: the local cemetery. Except something goes wrong and instead of raising just one or two of the dead, the entire cemetery bursts to life and masses of living corpses go to work feeding on the living.
Revolt of the Dead

When the lusty, enigmatic Nadezhta Zahorchak enters Bill's little life, everything goes right down the toilet. Bill begins having nightmares about Planet Mars. His friends begin to die. His favorite watering hole becomes a blood-soaked crime scene. And leggy, lipsticked vampires creep into the daylight to tear his world apart.
Anna Karnivora

LaVergne, TN USA
28 January 2010
171444LV00001B/26/P